THIS WALKER BOOK BELONGS TO:

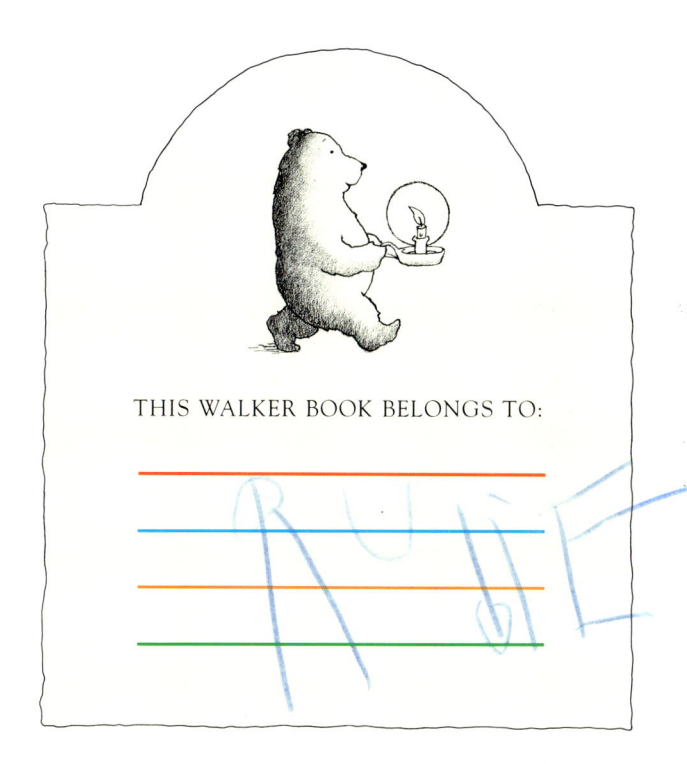

red nose readers

First published 1985 by Walker Books Ltd
87 Vauxhall Walk, London SE11 5HJ

This edition published 1990
Reprinted 1991, 1993, 1995, 1999, 2005

Text © 1985 Allan Ahlberg
Illustrations © 1985 Colin McNaughton

Printed in China

British Library Cataloguing in Publication Data
A catalogue record for this book is
available from the British Library.

ISBN 0-7445-1703-6

www.walkerbooks.co.uk

Blow Me Down!

Allan Ahlberg

Colin McNaughton

Blow Me Down!
Giant Days
Good Manners Gorilla

WALKER BOOKS
AND SUBSIDIARIES
LONDON • BOSTON • SYDNEY

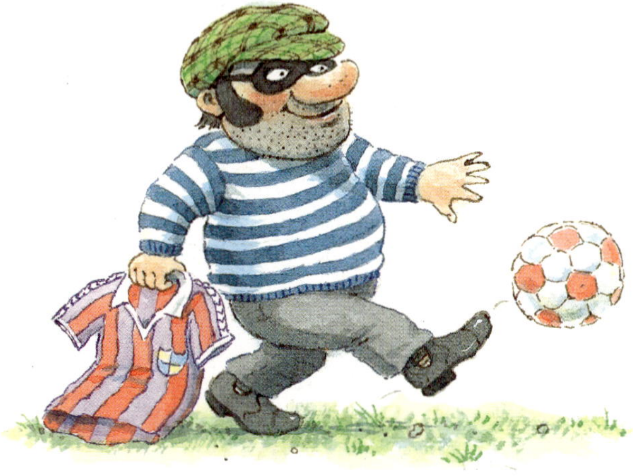

Blow Me Down!

'Blow me down!'
says Burglar Bert.

'Someone's pinched
my football shirt.'

'Blow me down!'
says Burglar Paul.

'Someone's pinched
my bat and ball.'

'Blow me down!'
says Burglar Pat.

A catastrophe!

'Someone's pinched
my pussy cat.'

'Blow me down!'
says Burglar Jake.

Crumbs!

Miaow!

'Someone's pinched
my birthday cake.'

'Blow me down!'
says Burglar Freddy.
'Someone's pinched
my bedtime teddy.'

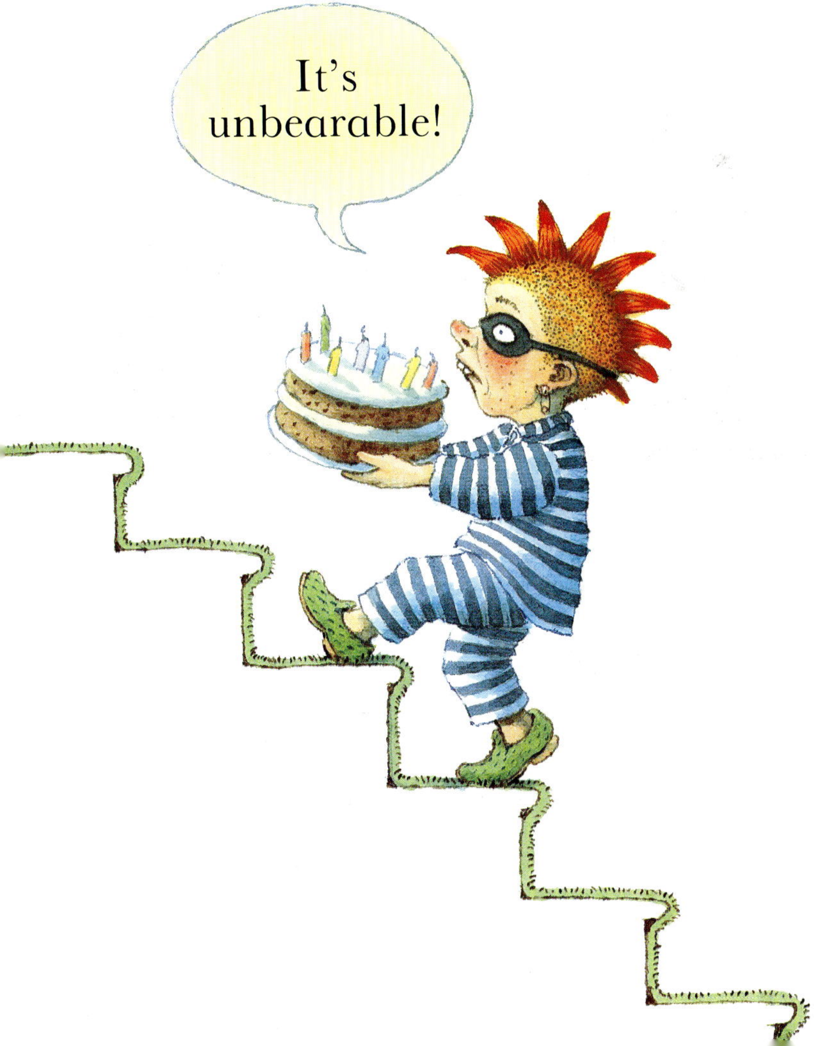
It's unbearable!

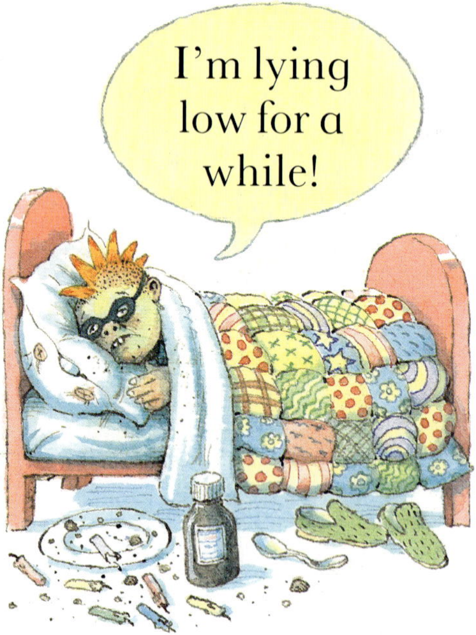
I'm lying low for a while!

Giant Days

In the days when giants walked the land,

they watched their step,
they lent a hand.

If you needed to move
to another town,

Which one?

a voice said, 'Which one?'
and an arm came down.

When clouds hung low
on your holiday,

a head appeared
and blew them away.

If you fell in the river
or lost your mum,

you just cried, 'Help!'
and help would come.

Yes, life was fun
and the weather was grand

in the days when giants
walked the land.

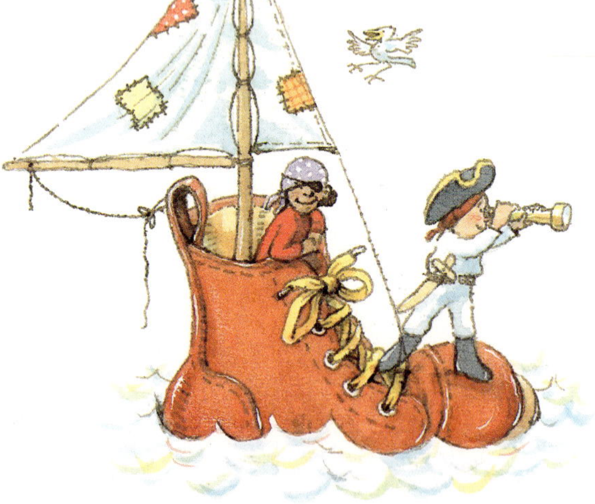

Good Manners Gorilla

When the good gorilla
  Comes to call,
Be sure to meet him
  In the hall.
Don't stick out your tongue
  Or snatch his hat.
He gets upset
  If you do that.

When the good gorilla
  Asks to see
How polite you are
  When you eat your tea,
Don't pick your nose
  Or play with the cat.
He gets upset
  If you do that.

When the good gorilla
>   Wants to check
That you always wash
>   The back of your neck,
Don't shout rude words,
>   Like 'blow!' or 'drat!'
He gets upset
>   If you do that.

When the good gorilla
 Says goodbye,
Be sure to have
 A tear in your eye.

Don't laugh like a drain
 Or roll on the mat.
He gets *really* upset…

... if you do that!

RED NOSE READERS

Allan Ahlberg / Colin McNaughton

Red Nose Readers are the easiest of easy readers – and the funniest!
Red for single words and phrases. Yellow for simple sentences.
Blue for memorable rhymes. How many have you got?

RED BOOKS

Bear's Birthday • Big Bad Pig • Fee Fi Fo Fum
Happy Worm • Help! • Jumping
Make a Face • So Can I

YELLOW BOOKS

Crash! Bang! Wallop! • Push the Dog
Me and My Friend • Shirley's Shops

BLUE BOOKS

Look Out for the Seals! • One, Two, Flea!
Tell Us A Story • Blow Me Down!

FOR THE BEST CHILDREN'S BOOKS,
LOOK FOR THE BEAR

www.walkerbooks.co.uk